ELENA THE FROG

The most glamorous dancing part is not always the most interesting – as Elena discovers in the ballet-school show.

Dyan Sheldon is a children's writer, adult novelist, humourist and cat lover. Her children's titles include *The Whales' Song* and, for Walker Books, *Sky Watching*, *A Night to Remember* and three stories about an alien cat and his human minder, *Harry and Chicken*, *Harry the Explorer* and *Harry's Holiday*.

Sue Heap has illustrated a number of children's books, including all three Harry and Chicken stories, and the picture books *Mouse Party*, *Little Chicken Chicken* and *Town Parrot*.

Books by the same author

Sky Watching

Harry and Chicken

Harry the Explorer

Harry's Holiday

For older readers

Ride on, Sister Vincent

Tall, Thin and Blonde

DYAN SHELDON

ELENA the FROG

Illustrations by Sue Heap

WALKER BOOKS
AND SUBSIDIARIES

LONDON • BOSTON • SYDNEY

For Patricia

First published 1997 by
Walker Books Ltd, 87 Vauxhall Walk
London SE11 5HJ

This edition published 1997

4 6 8 10 9 7 5 3

Text © 1997 Dyan Sheldon
Illustrations © 1997 Sue Heap

This book has been typeset in Garamond.

Printed in England by Clays Ltd, St Ives plc

British Library Cataloguing in Publication Data
A catalogue record for this book is
available from the British Library.

ISBN 0-7445-5407-1

Contents

Chapter One

Elena looked up as Sylvie's voice rose above the chatter in the changing room. "I wonder who Madame Maria's going to choose for the lead in the recital," Sylvie said.

She glanced at Elena. "It'll have to be someone who *looks* like a princess." She tossed her blonde hair. "My mother says I'm perfect for the part."

Elena kept her eyes on the
slipper in her hand.

Once a year the students of Madame Maria's School of Dance put on a ballet. This year the ballet was about a beautiful princess who couldn't find a husband. Then one day she kissed a frog. The frog turned into a handsome prince, and he and the princess lived happily ever after.

Madame Maria's School of DANCE

Elena wanted to be the beautiful princess more than anything in the world. She'd already seen the tutu she would wear. It was in the window of the dance shop. It was the colour of coral and sparkled with hundreds of silver stars.

It hadn't occurred to Elena that *Sylvie* might be given the part of the princess.

"You dance just as well as Sylvie does," Charlotte said. "You'd make a great princess and Sylvie knows it!"

"If I get the part, my mother's going to buy me a coral tutu covered with stars," announced Sylvie. She was practically shouting now.

When Elena heard the words "coral tutu", she turned round and stared at Sylvie in horror. *Her* tutu! Sylvie was going to dance in the recital in *her* tutu!

"My mother says I'll probably get a standing ovation," boomed Sylvie. Charlotte looked over at Elena. "I'd like to stand on *her* ovation," she said.

Chapter Two

The students of Madame Maria's School of Dance sat in a row on the floor of the studio while Madame Maria announced the parts for the class ballet. For once no one was talking. Not even Sylvie.

"Anna, Jasmine and Carl are the villagers," said Madame Maria. She cleared her throat. "Cleo and Kitty are the princes who have come to marry the princess, and Alan is the prince who was the frog."

Carl

Sylvie

Jasmine

Anna

Kitty

Elena sat beside Charlotte, holding her breath.

"Charlotte is the king," Madame Maria continued.

Charlotte puffed out her cheeks and shouted out, "Off with his head!" the way kings did.

Alan

Elena

Cleo

Charlotte

"Shhh," hissed Elena. Madame Maria was about to announce the princess. *Please don't let it be Sylvie*, Elena begged silently. She crossed all her fingers and toes.

"And Sylvie," boomed Madame Maria. "Sylvie shall be our princess."

Elena couldn't help herself. "But Madame Maria," she wailed. "Madame Maria, what about me?"

Madame Maria looked over at her. "You, Elena, shall be the frog."

Sylvie glanced over at Elena and gave her an enormous smile.

Chapter Three

Elena and Charlotte walked home together in silence.

"You shouldn't feel so bad," said Charlotte as they neared her house. "After all, the frog is the second biggest part in the ballet. The frog gets to dance almost as much as the princess."

Elena bit her lip, trying not to cry. She'd been so sure she would be the princess that she'd pictured herself leaping on to the stage a hundred times. She'd heard the audience gasp. She'd heard them begin to clap. She'd seen them stand up and cheer. "But I won't dance with the prince," she mumbled, "or in a coral-pink tutu."

Charlotte shrugged. "Being the frog is a lot better than being the king," said Charlotte. "All the king gets to do is pace back and forth."

"It just isn't fair," grumbled Elena.
"I bet Madame Maria only picked
Sylvie because she has blonde hair.
Princesses in fairytales always have
long blonde hair."

"They couldn't all have long blonde hair," argued Charlotte. "Some of them must have been dark." Charlotte made a face. "I bet she picked Sylvie because she already acts like a princess. She thinks she's so wonderful."

Elena kicked a stone out of her way. "I could dance even better than Sylvie if I wanted to," she said. "I know I could."

"So why don't you?" asked
Charlotte.

"No," said Elena, whacking
another stone into the gutter.
"If I can't be the
princess, then
I won't be in
the ballet
at all."

Chapter Four

"When are you going to tell Madame Maria you're not going to be the frog?" asked Charlotte as she and Elena took their places in the studio the next Saturday.

Elena leaned against the practice rail. "Right after class. When I can talk to her alone."

Sylvie was with Jasmine and
Anna at the other end of the rail.
Jasmine and Anna
were doing
their warm-up
exercises,
but Sylvie
was
practising
making
curtsies to
a cheering
crowd.

"My mother's going to give me a bouquet of flowers after the performance," Sylvie was saying loudly to Jasmine and Anna. "Just like a real *prima* ballerina."

"I'd like to give her something," whispered Elena.

"So would I," Charlotte whispered back. "Just like a real *prima* pain in the bum."

"My mother says I look just like a princess," Sylvie went on even more loudly. "Wait till you see me in my tutu."

Elena glanced over. Sylvie was tossing her hair and giggling with the other girls.

They're giggling about me, thought Elena miserably. *They're laughing because I don't look like a princess.*

Elena looked away.

But whenever Madame Maria mentioned the recital during practice, Sylvie glanced over at Elena and smiled. Sometimes she tossed her hair at the same time.

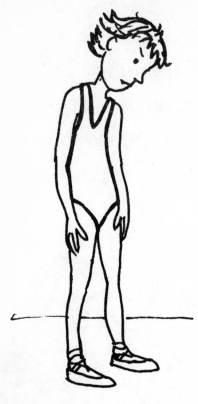

After the lesson, Elena hung behind. As she watched the other students leave the studio, she went over what she was going to say to Madame Maria. *I don't want to be in the recital*, she said silently. *I'm not going to be the frog.*

Madame Maria looked up and saw her. "Yes, Elena? Is there something you wanted to see me about?"

Elena was watching the doorway, where Sylvie, Jasmine and Anna were still talking in loud whispers. Sylvie said something to Jasmine and Anna, then glanced back and gave Elena an enormous smile. Jasmine and Anna laughed.

Suddenly Elena realized that Sylvie would be happy if Elena wasn't in the recital. She'd be glad someone who couldn't dance as well as her was playing the frog. She'd giggle with Jasmine and Anna about it. She'd shake her stupid hair and smile. "Poor Elena," she'd say, fluffing out the layers of the coral-pink tutu. "It's such a shame she doesn't look like a princess."

"Elena," said Madame Maria again. "Do you have something to say to me?"

Elena smiled. Charlotte was right. She'd show Sylvie. Elena might be a frog, but she was going to dance like a princess. She was going to outdance Sylvie, tutu or no tutu. Elena turned to Madame Maria. "No," she answered. "No, I don't have anything to say."

Chapter Five

Elena worked so hard at rehearsals, that even Madame Maria was impressed.

"Wonderful, Elena!" called out Madame Maria. "I do believe you're the best frog I've ever seen."

Only Sylvie wasn't impressed.

Whenever Elena got too close to her, she tried to trip her.

Whenever they passed each other, she tried to bump into her.

Whenever she could, she stepped
on her foot.

Elena worked even harder. She practised for her role as the frog every chance she got.

She spun through the kitchen.

She leaped through the living room.

She *pliéed* down the stairs.

She fluttered around the
bathroom.

She did *grands jetés* across the
back garden.

"You're a wonderful frog," said
Elena's mother as Elena soared over
the coffee table.

"That's pretty good," said Elena's father as she brought him his tea *en pointe*.

At rehearsals she leaped too high
for Sylvie to trip her.

She twirled too fast for Sylvie to
bump into her.

She danced across the imaginary lily pads too quickly for Sylvie to step on her foot.

"Excellent, Elena!" cried Madame Maria. "Excellent, indeed!"

Sylvie tapped her foot and scowled.

"Pay attention, Sylvie!" roared Madame Maria. "You've missed your cue again."

Elena glanced at Sylvie and smiled.

Sylvie didn't smile. "It doesn't matter how well you dance," she whispered to Elena. "I'll be the one in the coral tutu. Everyone's going to be looking at *me*!"

Chapter Six

The night before the recital, Elena dreamed that Sylvie had come down with a very bad cold and couldn't be in the ballet. Desperate, Madame Maria asked Elena to go on in her place. When she woke up, Elena could still see herself taking a bow while the audience applauded and cheered.

But when Elena arrived at the
auditorium, Sylvie was backstage,
looking like a princess in the coral-
pink tutu, glinting with stars.

Elena was just blinking back a
tear when Madame Maria herself
came rushing up to her. She had a
parcel wrapped in brown paper in
her hand.

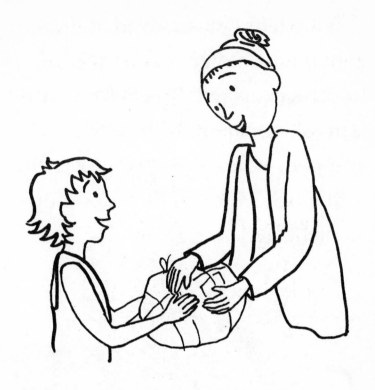

"Here," said Madame Maria, thrusting the parcel into her hands. "It's for you. For working so hard."

Inside the parcel was an emerald-green tutu, dusted with tiny gold moons.

When Elena leaped on to the stage in her emerald-green tutu the audience gasped. When she danced across the paper lily pads they clapped. When she sprang over the make-believe pond they stood up and cheered.

Everyone agreed
she was the best frog
Madame Maria's School of Dance
had ever had.

MORE WALKER SPRINTERS
For You to Enjoy

☐ 0-7445-3197-7   *A Night to Remember*
Dyan Sheldon/Robert Crowther   £3.99

☐ 0-7445-5258-3   *Care of Henry*
Anne Fine/Paul Howard   £3.50

☐ 0-7445-3188-8   *Beware Olga!*
by Gillian Cross/Arthur Robins   £3.50

☐ 0-7445-4111-5   *Oliver Sundew, Tooth Fairy*
Sam McBratney/Dom Mansell   £3.50

☐ 0-7445-4300-2   *Little Stupendo*
Jon Blake/Martin Chatterton   £3.50

☐ 0-7445-3091-1   *The Finger-eater*
Dick King-Smith/Arthur Robins   £3.50

☐ 0-7445-3095-4   *Millie Morgan, Pirate*
Margaret Ryan/Caroline Church   £3.99

Name _____

Address _____

_____